A Purr-poseful Passage:

To Where the Wind Howls Down

Be Inspired!
L. Claire Freeman

L. Claire Freeman

illustrated by Jacqui Freeman

authorHOUSE®

AuthorHouse™
1663 Liberty Drive, Suite 200
Bloomington, IN 47403
www.authorhouse.com
Phone: 1-800-839-8640

First published by AuthorHouse 12/5/2008

ISBN: 978-1-4389-2137-2 (sc)

Printed in the United States of America
Bloomington, Indiana

This book is printed on acid-free paper.

Cover design by Janelle Gonyea.

Dedication

This story is dedicated to Mimi, our city cat, Inky, our reservation cat, and my husband, Dave. Together and separately, they brought the vision of this story to life.

Acknowledgments

This story would not have evolved without the Native Americans of Montana, New Mexico and South Dakota. They took the time to teach us about and demonstrate their cultures during the time we worked on and lived as guests on their reservations. It was a profound experience that must be passed on, much like the Native tradition of story telling.

For their invaluable contributions to this story, I thank Shelley Freese, Robin Gerber, Kathy Kandt, Karen Yekel, and Jennifer Felts.

Chapter One

This story is about what happened to me and Terry. Others have told me about the parts that didn't include me directly, so I would be able to make sense out of the whole incredible adventure. I can't wait to pass it on to you, in the great storytelling tradition, so to speak.

Terry Littleman lived with his family in the country, but daydreamed of life in a big city. He longed for skateboard parks, 24-plex movie theaters, and cool cars zooming around. One day, when this 12-year old was given a special responsibility, he refused to do it. He blurted out hurtful words, saying he wanted only to get away from stupid and old-fashioned ways.

Terry's family became very worried about his reaction and gathered together for a meeting. Why was this job not an honor? They prayed for a way to help him, and finally, came up with an answer.

I am Mackenzie the cat, Mack for short, and our story begins with me and my family, way back on moving day.

Everyone stood calmly at the living room window, gazing out at the ocean waves one last time. They sighed at the beauty of the cityscape across the water. I, on the other hand, raced crazily around the house, leaping up and down on all the tall stacks of boxes in every room.

What was going on here? All the lamps and pillows and household decorations had disappeared! Why was the sofa all wrapped in plastic? Where was my scratching post? In a fit of panic, I lunged at the arm of a wrapped up chair.

"MACKENZIE! NO! BAD CAT!" shrieked Mom. June Butler turned back to the matters at hand.

"How is he ever going to ride in the car until we get there?" chimed in little sister, Julie. "And for three whole days!" added big brother, Jack.

Dad bent over me, and I began to purr nervously. "The cat may have to be left behind. You're lucky we even took you in, Mack, showing up at the back door as you did, and refusing to leave. There's so much you need to learn in order to be civilized, and I just don't have the time to teach you. Look at you now, racing around the house like you just ate catnip! Honestly Mack, this move is stressful enough. One of the neighbors said they'd take you." William Butler stood up with finality.

What he said was totally devastating. Left behind? No way! That neighbor kid was a brat who always pulled my tail. Besides, it took me forever to find this home. There's not much to say about where I lived before. I just had to leave, that's all. It's a cat thing sometimes... Distressed and brokenhearted, I ran to hide in the empty closet. There I sulked, with my chin on my front paws, and my ears perked.

"This will be a big change for us," I overheard Dad say with a worried tone. "You kids have never lived in snow before, nor in the kind of wind that howls down from the mountains."

SNOW . . . ? MOUNTAINS . . . . ? I buried my face in my long black fur.

I heard Dad go out to the garage, and put more stuff in the family car. Later I heard the roaring engine of a big truck, as it pulled up in front of the house. I saw three guys with KING'S TRANSFER AND STORAGE on their shirts take away all the boxes and furniture.

Dad's voice echoed in the empty room. "Okay, time for us to go. Julie, Jack, go find the cat."

Two pairs of hands yanked me out of the closet. As we stood before him, I wiggled in fright, dreading to hear whether I'd be 'transferred or stored'. He glared at me and said simply, "I'm warning you, Mack."

"PLEASE be good," Julie whispered, making my ear twitch. "We don't want to leave you behind."

"He'll settle down once we're on our way." Mom's voice sounded sweet and reassuring. She opened the car door and motioned to us. "Let's go!" Anxiously, everyone settled into their usual seats, and our family drove away.

I sat in the back window with front paws folded back, trying to act casual. All our well-known places faded away. All that remained the same was us, huddled together in the car, pointed toward the unknown. Mom passed around some popcorn, trying to make everyone feel like this was just another road trip. But it wasn't.

I suddenly remembered that in all the excitement, no one had fed me before we left. I was starving! Then again, I wasn't left behind, and I didn't want to make trouble. So, I yawned, and decided to just let the journey begin.

Chapter Two

The family car twisted and turned, weaving its way through bright green rolling hills. Houses and buildings became fewer and fewer. Then the land leveled out, and all I could see were miles and miles of newly planted farmland. The ocean was long gone, and nothing smelled like it should. I didn't want to look at any more strange scenery, so I moved down to the floor of the back seat.

Finally the car stopped. It was dusk. Mom mumbled something to me, but I wasn't listening. The doors opened and everyone hopped out. Unnoticed, I slipped out, too, and waited beneath the car until they were safely inside the restaurant.

I smelled REAL FISH, which was far more inviting than the bowl of fish shaped crunchies left for me on the dashboard. With caution, I made my way across the parking lot, stopping beneath each parked car along the way. The source of the smell became stronger and stronger as I reached a water's edge. There

I came upon a little old lady hunched over a fishing pole, her line dangling in the murky water.

"Well, hallo there kitty cat," she squealed in her high-pitched drawl. She wore a big brown cowboy hat and a fancy longhorn buckle on the belt of her jeans. She startled me when I noticed I was standing boldly out in the open.

"I bet you smelled my fish, you li'l dickens," she said, gleefully clapping her hands.

"Meow . . ." I answered in a tiny voice, saliva almost dripping off my starving lips.

"Okay sweet thing," and a tiny piece of bait flew in my direction. I leaped and downed the tasty tidbit in one gulp.

"Well mercy me! Where you from, blackie?" she asked, and tossed another minnow morsel near my whiskers.

"No collar, no food. Ain't you got a home darlin?" She stared at me curiously. I stared back, not knowing what to make of this fishing lady with the big hat.

"Yessiree, I sure could use a mouser for my barn." With one quick grab, she swept me up with her free arm, and gave me a possessive hug. I struggled and scratched, but was swiftly dropped into the cab of an old red truck.

"You got a home, now, Blackie!" She jumped in next to me and started the engine. We pulled away down a washboard gravel road, with fish and fishing pole bouncing in the back.

"MEEEOOOWWW," I wailed, but my cries were drowned out by the bump bang of the truck as it shuddered into the night.

The jerky ride seemed endless. Thunder began to rumble and I shook with dread as the old truck finally skidded to a stop "I'll put you to the barn tomorrow," mumbled the old lady, as she slammed the cab door and disappeared into the drizzly rain.

I looked all around me, but saw no way out. My teeth chattered with fear as I squinted between flashes of lightning, trying to see outside the blurred and grimy window. I was indeed all alone. Consoling myself with grooming, I nervously washed and smoothed my matted fur, hoping to scrub away the oily fish smell. How uncivilized, I thought. If only I'd stayed in the car!

I worried and worried about being separated from my family. I wasn't bad for being hungry, was I? Am I in big trouble now? Maybe they don't care that I'm lost! If only I knew where I was, or where to go to catch up...What a purr-fectly puzzling predicament!

I so wanted to be brave. At least it was warm and dry in the truck. Curling into a ball, I pulled my tail over my eyes to block out most of the jagged light. With a hopeful sigh I closed my eyes and willed myself to sleep.

Chapter Three

Meanwhile, back at the diner, my family returned to the car from their traveler's dinner, the kids happily calling for me as they swung open the back door. Of course, there was no answer. Happiness quickly turned to panic, as all of them turned over boxes and jackets, and Julie rattled the uneaten bowl of crunchies.

"Oh dear...," said Dad with a gulp of guilt. "Maybe I spoke too harshly to the cat and scared him away. I'm really fond of the silly fellow," he whispered with honest regret.

The quiet parking lot was pierced with frantic calls. They ran around everywhere. "MACK ... MACKENZIE .... HERE KITTY-KITTY!"

Only thunder answered in the distance. They found the riverbank, but no sign that their cat had ever been there. Julie and Jack began to cry. The sky began to tumble out a trail of rainy tears.

"Don't cry, children!" William Butler wrung his hands in helplessness. "Someone will find Mack and return him to us. I have to start my new job in a few days, and we just can't wait here any longer."

"But he has no collar," whimpered Julie. "He chewed them off twice!"

"Maybe he doesn't want to live with us anymore. Maybe he'd rather go back to where he was before." Jack felt more miserable in thinking any of this was true.

"Mack's out here somewhere. We'll just have to hope for the best!" Mom reached toward her brood for a comforting squeeze.

Saddened and rain soaked, they returned to the car. Without a word they drove off down the highway, to find lodging for the night, and to wait out the storm.

The next day the kids drew reward flyers. Mom and Dad put them up at many gas stations and rest stops along the highway. They described their cat to anyone who would listen.

"Ain't much chance of a city cat surviving around here," replied one discouraging local. "There're mountain lions and bobcats and other wild animals that would eat him up for lunch!"

Still, the Butler family had hope-- or blind faith- or whatever you want to call it. Even though two more days of traveling brought no sightings or clues to my fate, they wanted to believe that their wide-eyed, short-legged, clumsy, chubby little cat could find his way to them and their new home.

Chapter Four

The early morning sun blazed through the dew on the windshield of the old truck. "Wuf, Wuf!" barked an insistent furry face peering earnestly into the side door window.

Crouching, eyes narrowed to a slit, I glared back.

"Are you our new mouser?" asked the scruffy dog.

"I don't do mice!" I said. Wanting to appear confident, I briskly swished my tail. From the corner of my eye, I could see the dog was standing on a woodpile, so he couldn't be as huge as I first imagined. I was thankful, though, he was on the other side of the glass.

"A grandma type lady with a fishing pole and a big hat cat-napped me by a river. I'm supposed to be moving to a new home with my family, but she thought I was a stray. I'm no 'mouser'! All I've ever caught is a grasshopper in the backyard. My family probably thinks I ran away, but I was just hungry. Can't you see that I'm a city cat and don't belong here?" I collapsed back on the seat in a hopeless heap. "I just want to go home, wherever that is."

"What's your name, cat?" drawled his kindly voice.

"Mackenzie."

"Mac what?"

"Mack for short!" I corrected sharply.

"Whoa, you sure are a city cat, ain't you, fella?"

I frowned.

"Looky here, I can help you, Mack," replied the dog decidedly. "We ain't got much time, though. Aunt Sissy'll soon be up and about". He glanced back over his shoulder. "She'll set you to work right quick, and that'll be that. She don't take no for an answer, no matter how sweet she talks.

"Anyways, I can let you outta the truck, and take you to the end of this ranch. You'll have to find your own way from there. Aunt Sissy'll find another mouser. Yeah, I can see you ain't right for the job. Okay?"

For a brief moment I pictured my family out there somewhere in the car, getting farther and farther away. "Well, okay."

The smiley faced dog rattled the latch, and the truck door flew open. And I, with the courage of a cowardly lion, leapt down to freedom.

"So what's YOUR name?" I asked sincerely, trying to be friendly, and divert the fact that I was shaking in my puss' boots.

"Nipper."

"Nipper?"

"Yeah, that's my job! Nippin' at the heels of the cattle, makin' them go where they're supposed to. Don't be surprised if I get to nippin' at your heels, little fella," laughed the dog in friendly warning.

I smiled back, not knowing why I trusted this kindly cattle dog. He wasn't a big dog; more medium sized, even though he was more than twice as big as me. He looked kind of like a collie, with a permanently smiling mouth, calm eyes, and brown speckled hair. He was quite muscular and agile compared to me, who's more short and stocky with thick, clumsy paws. Most of all, he had a confidence I hoped to learn for myself.

It took Nipper many days to guide me safely through the cattle grazing range land.

"Stop lookin' back! Face straight ahead and let your nose lead the way!" he barked impatiently. "Don't step on cowpies and watch for them prairie dog holes!"

"I can't do this!" I finally whined as I stumbled along, my courage quickly waning. It didn't take long for one paw to get caught in a hole, while another squished.

"You'll never make it if you keep caterwauling! Now, get a grip!" The dog smirked to himself at his clever play on words. I was not smiling as I trudged on ahead, covered in dirt. There was little time for badly needed grooming, and the great outdoors was my 'as needed' litter box. No premium odor control here; just sun, wind, and lots of dust.

Nipper quickly noticed my struggle, but I took quite a while to see he had more important things in mind for me than comfort. His goal was to awaken my dormant instincts of hunting and survival, qualities rarely needed for city living, but very necessary for life in the wild. But, why, why did I have to do all this in the first place?

After many days of complaining, Nipper's repetitions finally sunk in and I began to identify some of the smells my nose picked up. Some scents seemed very familiar, and others completely new. The details are embarrassing, so I'll just say I learned the hard way not to chase a skunk. Likewise, I had only a couple of quills stuck in my nose before I knew to run from porcupines. Nipper had to stuff my mouth with leaves so he could pull the nasty things out. The leaves were to muffle my yowling, which unnerved him.

Speaking of leaves on a more pleasant note, Nipper pointed out many of the plants that grew around us. It was a welcome discovery to find burdock, which Nipper mashed up and put on my sores and rock cut paws at night.

"I smell Thanksgiving!" I proudly announced on another day.

"Oh, you mean this prairie sage?" Nipper pulled up a piece from the low lying bush, and held it in front of my nose. "There's lots of varieties. This one ain't the kind you put in your turkey stuffing. This one you boil up and use for an eye wash, like when the cattle kick up too much dust. Let's get goin', son." And off we went again, with Nipper reminding me constantly of both the dangers and the bounties of his beloved land. I became more excited each time I conquered another challenge. A city cat really could learn to live in the wilderness! Hooray for me!

Finally one day, long after the sun had faded into the purple and blue horizon, the cattle dog announced that we had reached the end of the ranch. He showed me that the creek we had been following much of the way was now no more than a trickle.

"Don't let that fool you, Mack. This time of year, the creeks can swell up before you know it. Look here. You can spend the night protected under this bush." Nipper crawled under to demonstrate how well he could be hidden.

"But how do I know where to go next?" I demanded in sudden alarm.

"Sleep on it. You've got enough learning to be on your way now, mister former city cat. I gotta get back to the cattle drive, or I'll lose my job!"

I wanted to cling to this cow dog I so admired, but knew he'd only nip at my heels. I simply shook my head, and thanked him for his invaluable lessons and genuinely caring company. "I'll never forget you, Nipper."

With a nod of his head, the grinning dog wished me a safe journey home, then turned and ambled back along the creek.

I dutifully slid under my tent-like bush, and soothed myself by repeating out loud all I could remember of what Nipper told me never to forget. "I can do this, I can do this," and purred myself into an anxious sleep.

At one point in the night, I woke from a terrible nightmare. I dreamed I was a two-legged cat and couldn't walk. I struggled to free myself from a cramped and tiny space. It felt awful. Trying to recover, I breathed slowly and looked up to the dark night sky. All the sparkling stars seemed to band together to form a protective shield over my leafy hideaway. Feeling wrapped in this glowing warmth, my nightmare vanished. A reassuring sense of safety helped me drop back into peaceful slumber on that first real night on my own.

Chapter Five

I woke up the next morning to the sound of snorting. I was startled to see hooves everywhere ... big ones, medium sized ones, and small ones. Looking up I saw HORSES . . . brown ones, gray ones, golden ones, spotted ones. A band of horses was busy eating the green grass in which they stood. None of them seemed concerned about me, and not a one kicked me.

"And who are you?" neighed a kindly grayish mare, as she nudged toward my refuge.

"Hello," I called out politely. "I'm one lost house cat. I've lost my family and my home, and I don't know where I'm supposed to go next. Nipper, the cattle dog, helped me get this far." As I slowly crawled out of my shelter, all the horses gathered around, and I related the story of how I got separated from my family.

"Is your name Mack?" asked a brown colt innocently.

"YES! How do you know that?" I was utterly astonished.

"Well," reported a honey colored yearling, "we watched this car stop by the side of the highway a couple times. These two kids got out and wailed their hearts out, 'Mack! Mack! We love youuu ... Here kitty kitty!' Then they got back in their car with two bigger people and drove off. They sure seemed determined."

"Which way did they go?" My heart was racing now.

"That way." The grayish mare vigorously shook her mane.

"And where are you all going?" I held my breath.

"That way, also, in the direction of the rising sun. It drenches the grass to make it grow thick and sweet in the mountains to the east. We'll come back down from there before the snow falls." The mare was very matter-of-fact, but seemed to hear what I was asking.

"Where is your home?" I wondered curiously, nodding to the entire herd.

"We are home, dear. We roam this land for many miles in each direction."

I suddenly remembered, "Excuse me, ma'am. The dad in my family told the kids they were going to live where it snows in the winter, and where the wind howls down from the mountains."

"That's a lot of places north and east from here," neighed a yellowish yearling.

"What about trees?"

"I don't know ......"

"Well, don't worry", began the reassuring mare, "we'll help you find your family. It certainly seems that they are looking for you, too. We can at least take you to the foot of the mountains."

"That would be great . . . but my paws hurt. They're better since Nipper's burdock, but I'm not used to this kind of land, and could never keep up. Thanks anyway. . ."

A spotted pony bent low. "This ground is indeed too rocky, even for us sometimes. Yes, it would be hard for you to keep up with our galloping pace. My name's Paint. Hop on my back."

"OKAY!" and with one leap, I landed with a thump.

"Now, hold on tight!" Paint stood up and took off, his mane whipping in the wind and slapping my face. I didn't care. "Wow, Wow!" Scared but thrilled, I hung on for dear life, hardly believing how fast we were moving.

I lost all track of time as I rode with this band of twelve horses. I quickly saw that Ms. Appy, an appaloosa, was the leader. There was no stallion. Patiently, Ms. Appy kept everyone in order, and told them what to do.

Paly, the golden palomino yearling, was sleek and fast. He reminded me of a Roy Rogers type western movie horse. Paint, my brown and white spotted carrier, never complained as he transported me around. "You're like a little backpack, Mack! No problem at all."

Everyone soon let me know that life was not easy on the open range. Ms. Appy had many problems to solve. The region had suffered bad drought conditions. It was a constant test of endurance for her to find enough water, green grass, and shelter.

As a meat eater, I was encouraged to eat what I could catch in rodents, bugs, birds, and occasional fish. It was difficult, but thanks to Nipper and lots of practice, I reawakened my feline abilities to track, ambush, and pounce. No one handed the horses a bucket of oats and an apple, either.

"After all," said Nipper and Ms. Appy repeatedly, 'our survival is at stake, so we must do what we must do'.

Besides finding enough food, the horses were constantly watching for natural enemies. I was surprised one day when we took off running, not because we were being chased by a mountain lion, but by cowboy wranglers! Galloping with tails held high, we raced across the rocky terrain, the older ones protecting the younger ones from twirling lassos.

"They're always trying to round up another bucking horse for their rodeos," shouted Paint indignantly above the roar of the pounding hooves. "Or, they want to make us cutting horses for their ranches. We just want to be free to roam. This land is our home," and he pushed even harder to gain more speed. Thankfully, no one got captured that perilous day.

Another day there was a sudden cloud burst, and Ms. Appy screamed, "FLASH FLOOD! High ground. NOW!" We all took off again, hooves splashing mud everywhere. My fur got soaked as blinding sheets of rain hammered our backs. Side-stepping rocks and gullies, the sprinting steeds climbed the hillside in record time. I buried my face in Paint's muddy mane, and cringed at the sound of the roaring currents. The tumbling water fanned fiercely in every direction, sweeping away rocks and even trees that stood in its path.

Just as suddenly as it began, the rain stopped, and rainbowed rays lit the landscape once more. I peeked from my perch to see blue skies and sun. The herd took one look at my dazed scowl, and whinnied with laughter. Paly trotted over and tried to console me with an affectionate nudge. "We're used to this, Mack, but we know that you're not. You were very brave." The others snorted and pawed the ground in agreement. Once again, I trusted I was in good hands, er ... hooves, and everything would be all right.

Some lazy afternoons when the warm sunlight put everyone in a contented mood, the horses rubbed their heads against one another for affection and a sense of security. It reminded me how much I missed my family as I watched them play. The foals tried to nuzzle me, but even they were a bit too big. They pushed me over so many times I was overcome by fits of giggles. It was a welcome diversion to the seriousness of life in the wilderness. I wondered once again why I had to endure all of this.

I missed sitting on a lap, being brushed and petted and hugged and kissed, as only humans can do with their pets. As I looked around, though, I felt less and less like someone's pet. I wasn't sure what that meant, but held onto it. I appreciated the wonderful company of my equine friends, who somehow made me feel stronger and wiser, just as Nipper did.

When I just about believed I had turned into a horse myself, Ms. Appy announced we had reached the base of the mountains. "We're going to leave you here, Mack. There are no human families in the grassy valleys where we are going. Your chances are better if you seek your family from here."

Heart pounding, I jumped down from Paint's back for the last time. The herd encircled me, neighing their goodbyes as they nudged me good luck. I returned a thousand "thank yous." Before I might lose courage, Ms. Appy gave the signal, and the band galloped away and soon out of sight.

I stood there and looked all around the lonely landscape, finally spotting a small cave where I might spend the night. Imitating a whinny and a gallop, I sprang to my bed, purring with pride at the progress I had made. Me, Mack, a backyard city cat, was now a wilderness traveler. Too tired to hunt for supper, I chuckled to myself, "Sure would be nice to just pop a can." And before I knew it, I dozed off into dreamland.

Chapter Six

That night, I dreamed about mountains of cans of cat food . . . turkey and tuna and liver and chicken and chunky beef. Next to them were big bags of crunchy snacks, all neatly stacked in a kitchen pantry.

"I don't like to have to hunt for food" I muttered in my sleep. "It's too hard and not any fun . . ."

"But we all have to eat!" answered a squeaky voice hidden outdoors. "This is the wilderness and we have to catch our food."

"What?" I jerked myself awake. "Who said that?" I looked around in the dark, but all I saw were many pairs of eyes blinking back at me. "Who are all of you?"

"We are all the animals of this earth," spoke many voices at once. "We want to tell you that we forgive you if you must hunt us for food. Likewise, we ask you to forgive us if we someday catch you.

"We are all on this earth together, as plants and animals and bugs and all living things. Sometimes, we must be generous and kind and help each other in times of need. Most of all, we must be thankful for the gift of food."

"All right," I stuttered humbly, not knowing quite what to make of these voices. "Nipper was generous and helped me, and so were the horses. I am truly thankful and grateful for them."

As I spoke, all the blinking pairs of eyes seemed to join with all the blinking stars in the night sky. Slowly it all began to make sense. I felt surrounded by a kind of peacefulness, a togetherness with the universe as a member of a large family.

"WOW! I get it. I am not alone at all..." With that aware-ness, the blinking disappeared, and I woke up looking forward to a new day.

Chapter Seven

After giving thanks and appreciation for my hunted break-fast, I danced along, feeling light-hearted with a renewed sense of purpose and direction.

Upon discovering a great river, I closely followed a tributary, first to the right, then another to the left. This went on for several days. Doubt set in. Had I gone anywhere? There just seemed to be more water, with no end in sight. My paws were caked with mud. I hollered and yowled to keep myself company, but it didn't make me feel any less lost.

Rounding a bend in the shoreline, I came upon a large brown and green turtle. He appeared to be sitting there waiting for something. "Well, hello there cat!" He nodded cheerfully. "I've been waiting for you to get here."

"You have? Why?"

"I heard your lonely laments in the currents of the water and the wind. Where are you going? How can I help you?"

"I don't know. . ." How foolish I felt. "I'm just trying to find my family's new home. I'm not sure how you can help me, Mr. Turtle. Don't you just swim around in the water all day?"

"Yes, I live here where the water flows. Water is very powerful medicine! When the currents pull me steadily along, I feel in harmony with all of nature. Because I carry my house around with me, I am home wherever I am. I never feel out of sorts. Say, are you 'Mack', the missing family cat?"

I twitched nervously, totally shocked to hear my name spoken for the second time by complete strangers. "What makes you ask?"

"Well, often I sit here quietly sunning myself by the water's edge. The sparrows and meadowlarks and woodpeckers all stop by to visit and tell me the news of this region. They told me the other day that someone's cat had been lost. They heard people at rest stops reading flyers, and chirped the word along to watch out for a 'chubby, little, long haired black cat, dead or alive.' You fit the description. No other city cats have been sighted, and you're quite alive!"

"Yeah, that's me, and I'm still lost . . ."

"Well, Mack, why don't you come swim along with me for awhile?"

"But, it's getting dark out," I whined.

The turtle chuckled. "I'd enjoy the company, and you just might get closer to your family! We may have a lot in common. My name is Ernest Swimsalong, because that's what I do. Call me Ernie!" He lumbered into the water and waved for me to join in.

Doing some quick thinking, I decided this large and friendly turtle did not want to hurt me. He seemed sincere in his generous offer to help me. I couldn't say no to following him into the water unless I tried it, but what could we possibly have in common? How could the water make me closer to my family?

"I don't remember how to swim, Ernie."

"Come on, Mack! It's like riding a bicycle. It all comes back. You never forget."

"But I've never ridden a bicycle!"

"Oh, you know what I mean!" and he began to paddle away.

"Wait!" I jumped off the bank. At first it was a struggle, and I got pulled under by one too many currents. "I can't do this," I gasped, spitting out another mouthful of water. "PLEASE help me get out!"

"You must not fight with the power of the water, Mack." With patience and sureness, Ernie swam over to help. "Hold on to my shell until you get the hang of it. I won't let you drown." Slowly and steadily he took off paddling again with me in tow.

After the first few days, I began to have fun. Some days when the water flowed too swiftly, Ernie floated on his back while I rode on his belly. Other days, gliding side by side, we made parallel lines in the water as we drifted along. We entertained ourselves by making up silly names for the cloud shapes overhead. The water felt fresh instead of frightening now, and the air was filled with the pungent odors of the soil and the plants that lined the riverbank.

I couldn't believe how easy and pleasant it became to talk with Ernie. It seemed like I'd known him all my life, and could be happy making a home here by the river, forever. I felt a deep trust and joyfulness I had not felt before. Even the local waterfowl and other feathered creatures dared to perch nearby to warble and honk the news of the day. Although I could, I did not need to hunt them down for food.

"You know, Mack, I sense that you are beginning to notice that "home" is also a feeling you carry around daily in your heart. You are quiet and content around all these birds! A warm feeling of affection often grows slowly and steadily until it stays with you forever. Maybe this is part of what you've lost, and are beginning to find again."

"Oh, Ernie, I was truly sad to be separated from my family, but elated to find out how much they want me back! I am forever grateful for what Nipper taught me about hunting and surviving in the wilderness. I wanted to roam with the horses forever, and now I want to swim with you forever. I know I will never lose any of these experiences. They are wonderful feelings of friendship I can carry in my heart always.

"Most of all, when I need to, I can always see the face of "home" in my heart. It looks just like a turtle shell, with your funny face on top winking back at me. Thank you so much, Ernie, for helping me see more than ever before that I am closer to my family and our new home."

"Sounds like we can go on to the island now, Mack."

An island seemed like a curious place to go. We took off as thunder rumbled in the distance, and the water began to churn up. Arriving just before a hailstorm, we sought shelter in a cluster of rocks with a very long overhang. For the next two days we gave thanks and appreciation for the enjoyment of both good company and several fish and water lily dinners.

Then I had another nightmare. I dreamed I was a tearful little kid who could only meow. Telling Ernie about it the next day, he said that sometimes spirits in strange disguises talk to us in dreams. "Hmm, a mystery." Changing the subject he asked, "How will you know when you've reached home?"

"I already told you there would be snow or the mountains or the howling wind, Ernie."

The turtle nodded and pointed. "The wind comes over those mountains, and blows down slope. Your family could easily be on this side of the mountains somewhere. It may not be long until you find them."

My heart pounded with excitement.

"Well my friend, I believe you are ready to continue on your own. The water is calm again and you can be on your way," he said.

"You're going to leave me alone? Here?"

"There may be something more here for you to discover. You have adapted well to the ways of the water, so you should be fine. I have faith in you, Mack. Do come to visit me again someday."

I reached out to hug my roly poly companion. Although I had a stomach ache, I knew I could do as he instructed. I did not doubt his judgment. "Thank you, Ernie," and I watched him waddle back into the water, wave, and float off downstream.

Alone once more, I turned round and round in a circle, and finally settled down. Better tidy up, so I groomed and thought, and thought and groomed, deciding on first things first. Finally resolving that 'curiosity would not kill the cat,' I stood up. With courage and confidence I set out to explore this peaceful looking environment.

Chapter Eight

It was difficult to decide which way to go. I had utmost trust in Ernie's instructions, so I just marched along, totally caught up in recounting our conversations. Consequently, I didn't notice that following me, were several figures who were partially concealed in the brush.

Upon entering a small clearing, a low warning growl made me stop short. The hair on my back raised, my tail puffed up, and my eyes widened with alarm. A lone, dark animal shape shirked into view. Then there was another and another, four in all, closing in around me. They were coyotes! Oh no!

Out of the corner of one terrified eye, I saw a nearby tree. If I could just jump into it, they wouldn't get me! In an instant I lunged, only to be stopped by a snarling set of teeth that sunk into my neck, knocking out all breath.

"HELP . . . help . . ." I heard my tiny voice plead from far, far away. A taunting high pitched screech seemed to answer, and a huge, shadowy figure showed up beside me. The coyotes suddenly scattered. A throbbing neck pain followed me into unconsciousness.

When I woke up, I heard singing and smelled a sweet smoke. My neck, face and cheek were heavy with some kind of mud or paste. Upon opening my eyes, I stared into the cloudy face of another much larger cat.

"Hello, my brother," greeted a voice deeper than mine.

I blinked my eyes, but did not move nor make a sound.

"You have come back. You will be all right now." It was a strong and soothing tone. "I have been singing all last night and all this day, that it would not be your time to stand before the Creator. This sweetgrass smoke has taken up my prayers."

My eyes turned toward the haze of spiraling smoke. All I could do was nod my heavy head.

"I believe the red earth paste has helped to heal your wounds. Try to get up. Those coyotes won't hurt you anymore. I chased them straight over an old buffalo jump nearby." His eyes twinkled.

Recalling the intense pain that put me down, I was very guarded in getting up. Slowly lifting my head, I was surprised to feel fairly light, except for the weight of the red mud. There was no pain. The big cat nodded with satisfaction.

"Come over to the river. Let's wash off the red earth and see."

I didn't feel threatened by this other cat, even though he was at least three times my size. His fur was neither long nor short, and was a kind of light tan color with darker tones of spots and stripes. His ears seemed big for the size of his head and face.

He walked with powerful strides, and had extra large paws compared to me. Why did he want to help me?

I followed him over to the shore, and obediently dipped my paws into the familiar water. I couldn't feel any wounds, but jumped back when I saw my reflection shimmering back at me.

"Ah...yes! You have a gift. The Great Spirit has marked you with a white patch, so you will never forget this day."

In place of my all black hair, there was now a small white patch of fur at my throat. It did not come off no matter how hard I rubbed. "Who are you?" I stammered uneasily.

"I am your brother the bobcat. I came as soon as you called me for help. I have been guarding you since the attack. It's the least I could do for a brother in need. I am always around."

"But I am just a housecat, a stranger to this wilderness."

"We are both the same in the eyes of the Creator. I am your Guardian Spirit. The Creator is watching over you through me. It is my job to bring you the peace of mind that you are protected."

"If I stay out here, will I become a bobcat like you?"

"No, you must be yourself, as the Great Spirit intended. Do you know who that is?"

"I am already very different from when I first became lost. I've just been trying to find my home and my family. All these strange experiences have changed everything. Now I don't even look the same. Maybe when I find my family, I can feel like myself again. I am so close to the right mountains. Can you help me get the rest of the way home? Do you know which direction will take me there?"

"You must go in all four directions to make it home, my brother."

"But, but, I have already gone every which way", I hollered, my patience wearing thin.

"You will recognize that each direction has its own powerful teaching. There are spirits in the four directions that guide us to make good choices for a happy life. Do you think you would have made it this far without them?"

"I don't know . . ."

"All right, little one, I will show you. You have already gone East, toward the rising sun. It is the power of the sun's energy that encourages all life to grow and mature. Did the horses encourage you as they guided you to the foot of the mountains?"

"For sure! Say, how do you know about the horses? Were you there?"

"Yes, and 'every which way' of your journey. It has only been here that you have called for my help."

"So that is what Ernie meant . . . You are the 'something more' for me here."

The bobcat nodded and continued. "Your journey with Nipper at the very beginning . . . Did he help you grow more mature and gain confidence and endurance with all that he taught you or showed you?"

"Oh yes! He showed me how blind I was to surviving in the wilderness. I wouldn't be here today without him ... or you!"

"And that is South. Now, you have just come from going West. You met Ernie and the power of the flowing waters. Flowing waters of the land and falling water in storms are sacred gifts from the Creator. You learned the power of water with the horses, too."

"For sure!"

"You have only to go North to complete your passage."

"How do you know all this, bobcat?"

"I have guided many passages of many lifetimes, my brother. It is a wisdom that comes with age."

"That must be something like guiding someone through all nine lives. I must have used up at least one of those on this journey so far."

I somehow could relate to what the bobcat meant better than I understood it in literal words. I did feel closer to home and something must have helped me. So, okay, "What should I do next, Mr. Bob? I hope it's all right to call you that."

"Whatever helps you, my brother. To go North you will follow the shoreline around to the left. You'll see a narrow place where you can wade across to the mainland again. Watch where the sun goes to see which way is North. You've done so well to make it this far and now you have only to finish."

I reached out to touch Mr. Bob in a gesture of thanks, but merely swatted air. I saw a distinct bobcat, but it had no physical form.

"I'll be seeing you, Mack," and he was gone.

I sat where I was for a long while, feeling very, very confused. Was I really almost killed? Did my wounds make me delirious and imagine 'spirits'? And what about my nightmares? Spirits and disguises? .... What was real and what was not? None of the directions in which I had gone had been without new learning and new feelings. I was about to burst with weariness at the thought of more. What did going North mean? What else did I have to learn? I was just a cat trying to get home. Why did I have to go through all this other stuff to get there?

"Oh, stop feeling sorry for yourself and quit complaining," said a faraway voice inside me. "Yes, it's more and more lessons to learn. Now, get up!" said the voice.

Wow, where did that come from? I jumped up and looked around, but saw no one. Cautiously I crept back down to the water. The white patch was still at my throat. Shrugging, I turned and dutifully padded in the direction I was told to go. I found the shallow place and started crossing to the other side. Suddenly, my legs wouldn't work. I wanted to go left, but my legs moved to the right.

"Left!" I commanded aloud. "I don't want to go right because the land is riddled with steep cliffs and the left isn't!"

Why was my mind fighting with my paws? After making no progress and stumbling face first into the water, I finally gave in. "Okay, right it is," I gurgled, and the struggle stopped. Frowning, I scanned the area and spotted a suitable ledge on which to sleep, all the while eyeing the dense and sumptuous shrubs that promised a much more protective shelter to the left.

That night I heard all kinds of threatening animal sounds and shivered. Were they spirits or were they real? Then a sudden warm breeze reminded me of the comforting presence of the bobcat's protection. "Thank you," I whispered, and turned round and round on my perch to settle into a comfortable spot. Before curling up to sleep, I gazed up at the rising man-in-the-moon. I knew he would cast a watchful eye over my bed. Only North now. I sighed and fell asleep.

Chapter Nine

At dawn, way, way up in the sky, two eagles circled over-head. "SCREE, SCREE!" they called to each other, and swiftly swooped low.

"A fine meal!" the female cawed.

"Yes, an easy prey!" the male answered with a final dive to my ledge.

Before I knew what was happening, I was lifted up by the scruff of my neck and carried high in the sky. In a flash I sized up what was happening, and shouted in the wind, "Bobcat, help me now, PLEASE!"

"You must trust this time, little brother," returned the low pitched voice in the wind, and I knew he wasn't going to rescue me. While the end of my life flashed before me, a calm voice seemed to flow out of my throat.

"Oh great eagles, you fly higher than any other birds," I heard myself say. "Please take a prayer up to the Great Spirit for me.

I can see now that I will never make it home." I was amazed at the calmness and clarity of the words coming out of me.

Was it really me talking? The words continued to flow.

"I am truly thankful for the help of Nipper the dog, Ms. Appy and her herd, Ernie the dear old turtle, and the guardian bobcat. They all helped me get this far when I felt so lost.

"Please find a way to let my family know that I almost made it home. Although I will dearly miss them, we will forever be together in our hearts..." I closed my eyes to accept my fate, as we landed on a ledge way up high on a rock wall.

"Scree, scree," echoed the black and white feathered couple. Their keen eyes pierced my very core. "We can see that you have been learning many lessons of life. We respect your journey."

"You do?" I was stunned.

"We would be honored to take your prayer up to the Great Spirit. However, it would be a greater good for you to learn the reason for your efforts. How can we help you find your family?" Both eagles flapped their magnificent wings and waited.

I stammered, "I need to find a place where families live, where it snows and where the wind howls down from the mountains." My request sounded impossible as I gestured toward the vast peaks surrounding us.

"The Creator has given us the gift of flying high in the sky, so we can survey the land below. If you will let us carry you, we will fly North and see what we can find." They fluttered and bobbed their white feathered heads.

"Oh yes!" I blurted, with every inch of grateful fur. Without delay they lifted into flight once again, with a very eager passenger.

It took a while for me to get used to flying like a bird. Then again, wasn't it only yesterday that I had been galloping on the back of a horse, and swimming on the shell of a turtle? Surely flying was just another purr-poseful challenge.

The view from the sky made me dizzy, as the strong winds pushed us higher and higher. The temperature plummeted. "Is that snnooooww?" I said, teeth chattering with cold.

"Those are the last of the glaciers that used to cover most of this region millions of years ago. As long as it stays cold, they will likely never melt." Mr. Eagle was very informative.

"Wwhheerrree arrre the treeees?" I asked, still shivering. There was just rock with tall peaks.

"We are above the tree line. We will fly lower soon and the terrain will change."

And change it did as we progressed along. Suddenly there were pine trees and leafy trees and green valleys and meadows filled with wildflowers. "And what's that water? Look at it glisten!" I flashed on how far away the ocean must be.

"Some are rivers and streams, some are glacial lakes, and some are prairie potholes, as the locals call them. We'll stop for the night soon, and must be very careful where we land to rest.

"We assume that you already know how to identify black and grizzly bears, bobcats, coyotes, mountain lions, moose, elk, bighorn sheep, wolves, and even some bison that live off this land. You must have seen or met up with most of these animals during your time in the wilderness."

"Well, yes, some, but...."

"To be safe, we will be stopping only at the nests of relatives." Mrs. Eagle was very emphatic.

And stop we did at least twice a day to rest, visit relatives, and hunt for food. I appreciated the fact that we ate much of the same cuisine, and enjoyed several community picnics. I learned that Mr. Eagle's name was Skyler, and Mrs. Eagle's, Skyla. They referred to me as Mack, and I called them Skyler and Skyla from then on.

"I don't see many houses," I observed on another day.

"Yes, along this area there are mostly ranches and a lot of open space. We'll still pass a few towns."

We did pass over a few small towns, but none of them caught my attention enough to land. Pressing on, we reached a place where smells preceded the presence of people. There was an inviting fragrance of wildflowers that blanketed the prairie below. There was the mouthwatering odor of campfires and cooking that drifted through the brisk air.

The wind roared down off the mountains to our left. White snowy dots and jagged peaks loomed above the small town beneath them. As we got closer, I saw animals, people, and many colors moving around in some kind of activity.

"Let's go there!" I pointed with an excited paw.

"Indeed," replied the soaring pair as they surveyed the territory. "We cannot take you all the way to town, but we can drop you off on the prairie just outside."

"That will be fine!" I couldn't explain the strange feeling I had as we neared the ground.

"If this is not the right place, call for us, and we will hear your plea on the wind," instructed Skyler.

"And come get you to take you further," added Skyla, as we landed in a field of purple. "So we will not say goodbye here, Mack. We never like to say goodbye, anyway. If nothing else, we will meet again one day as we all stand before the Great Spirit. For now we will say 'see you.'"

They both flapped their huge expanse of wings and lifted off.

"Thank you, see you!" I called upward, watching them make higher and higher circles in the sky.

Chapter Ten

Anticipation grew as I trekked toward the activity of town. Although my flight with the eagles had been thrilling, I was really glad to be back on solid ground again. My walk through the delicately scented purple and pink and yellow and red and white wildflowers was intoxicating. Looking up, I noticed the deep blue sky and the huge, fluffy clouds. I sighed with contentment.

As I approached the crowds, I dived under a platform so I wouldn't get run over. I watched and listened. There was some kind of rhythmic drumming and singing. Many adults and children were dressed in colorful cotton or leather clothes decorated with feathers, beads, shells, or bells that jingled as they danced to the drumming. There were painted faces and painted horses. Some horses had hand crafted halters and blankets.

A cluster of painted tipis was set up against the base of the mountains, where the wind howled down. Darting around hooves and feet, I weaved my way over to them. As I got closer, they appeared much larger than expected. Long and narrow pine trees, stripped of bark and dried, formed the shape of the painted canvas that wrapped around them.

Seeking shelter from the wind, I ducked into the only tipi with an open flap. It was dim inside, but a small fire in the center shimmered as it sent smoke curling up and out the hole at the top. An old man was quietly sitting alone.

"Excuse me, sir," I meowed politely. Oh, but could he speak cat? Boldly I continued. "I am Mack, a house cat from a city. I lost my family and have been on what seems like a very long journey to find them. They are four: William and June, the parents, and Julie and Jack, the children."

"Oki poesco (Hello cat). We have been waiting to see if you would make it here."

"What?" I was taken aback by the voice. And was he speaking cat or was I speaking human . . . No matter. Just another purr-plexing experience!

"On this long journey of yours to find your family, you helped one of our Native sons to find his home, also."

"I did?"

"My grandson, Terry, longed to move to a modern city to get away from what he thought were his family's embarrassing and old-fashioned ways. His father had been the leader of our clan society, and his job was to lead us in upholding our long-standing beliefs and traditions at various ceremonies throughout the year.

Terry's father suddenly died last year, and his special job was to be passed on to his son. We were shocked when Terry didn't want the responsibility of the job, and deeply saddened by his hurtful words that said our old customs and ceremonies had no place in the modern world. He turned his back on the bobcat that had been chosen as his lifelong Spirit Guide.

We could see that Terry was suffering from not only the loss of his father, but many other issues as well, and we felt helpless in reaching out to him. We all agreed that Terry had lost his sense of belonging to the sacred spirit of our people. So the elders of our clan gathered to pray to the Great Spirit for guidance on such a serious matter. They had a vision that a white man's city cat should carry the spirit of the boy. Circumstances dictated that both were to be left to find their own way."

"OH, OH," I said excitedly. "So I didn't really have nightmares. The two legs and not being able to meow were Terry! It was he who spoke so seriously to the eagles. The bobcat defined the four directions for him!" I was breathless with excitement, and a little confused.

"And absolutely for you, too, poesco. Not everyone can communicate with the creatures of this earth. As you learned humility and respectfulness, they were able to help you. Terry was unable to do that. You helped him reconnect with the importance of his spirit brothers. You far exceeded our expectations by finding an appreciation for all your lessons. Without realizing it, you encouraged and enabled Terry to embrace his culture again!"

"I did?"

"The best part of all is that Terry didn't know if his body was trapped inside yours, or that your spirit inhabited him. It didn't much matter because you both had a marvelous sharing of experience anyway. We were all thrilled, delighted, and amazed at the outcome of this merging."

"You were?"

"You both adapted to a different world than you were used to. You allowed the experiences of the Four Directions to demonstrate the virtue in our beliefs. By learning Courage, Patience, Endurance, and Quick Thinking, you brought honor to yourself while showing Terry how to respect them again. Through you, Terry reunited with his Bobcat Guardian Spirit. And now, you have earned the Gift of the Bobcat watching over his brother 'poesco', also. We are proud and grateful for what you have accomplished on this journey."

"Well, I'm still a bit confused, but I think you are saying I helped Terry believe in the values of his home and his people, while I sincerely tried to find my home and people, too. What a wonderful purr-pose to this trip ... a true passage to find the meaning of 'home'. You know, your manner and your voice remind me so much of my dear friend Ernie, the turtle, whom I met along the way."

"My name is Leonard, little one."

"Grandfather Leonard, I will never forget all that has happened, especially the friends that generously helped me and Terry along the way. I can see now that it was Terry who helped me keep going, too. I feel so different from before. Just look at the white patch at my throat. Can I ever again be just an ordinary housecat? But Grandfather Leonard, I need to find my family again. Can you help me do that?"

"Yes, poesco. First, the elders wish to honor you. They have chosen a new name which recognizes the success of your passage." Leonard motioned, and five other elders entered the tipi.

I rubbed my eyes, and shook my head as the flickering fire lit their faces. There was Nipper and Paint and Mr. Bob and Skyler and Skyla and, of course, Ernie, all smiling back at me. Was I imagining this?

Their high-pitched voices began to sing aaya, aa, ya, accompanied by the beat of a low pitched, decorated drum. They sang prayers of thanksgiving, sent up to the Great Spirit through the spiraling smoke of the fire. I recognized the same prairie sweetgrass smell from my time with the bobcat. I thought it must be very special. That evening my wide-eyed, short-legged, clumsy, chubby little self named Mackenzie, became "Nahtotse Nesemoo" (my pet, the familiar helping spirit).

"May you always remember the wisdom of this journey," barked Nipper.

"We are honored to help you rejoin your family," whinnied Paint.

"And live an everyday life again," purred Mr. Bob.

"You have done so well, we ask if we may call upon you to help us again some day," screeched Skyler and Skyla.

"Of course!" I roared, then caught my breath . . .

Leonard tapped me on the shoulder with a beautifully carved bone staff. The next thing I knew, I was sitting by the back door of a house that faced the mountains. The wind howled under the eaves.

Jumping up on a window sill, I peered inside the house. There were the old familiar chairs and lamps and pillows, and even my old scratching post.

"MACK!" came a sudden scream from Julie, who ran to open the door.

"Mack, oh Mack!" yelled Jack, as he pushed on past her and scooped me up in his arms. He squeezed me so hard I squeaked!

William and June rushed outside, too, and all gushed at once:

"I knew you could find us!"

"Where have you been?"

"Are you okay?"

"Are you hungry?"

"You look all in one piece, but what's that white spot? Is it really you, Mack?"

"And what do you have to say for yourself?" asked William, as he bent over me and gently stroked my head.

I purred and purred and kneaded Jack's chest. "It's really me," I meowed. "What a journey I have been on, with so many helpers along the way."

Would they ever know how I had forever changed, other than the white patch that wouldn't rub off. Well, that's enough explanation for now. Jumping down, I ran inside and went straight to my old familiar scratching post. Ahhh, home at last.

Chapter Eleven

At the same time I found myself at the back door of my family's home, a 12-year old Native American boy found himself standing before the elders in the tipi. Still disoriented, he stood quietly and stared at the men around the campfire.

"Oki, my son. You made it back. I had faith you would come back home."

"Grandfather!" the young man shouted with recognition, as he reached out to hug him. "I am home, and so glad to be back."

"Do you remember what happened, Terry?"

"Yes . . ." Recollection began to flood in . . . "You sent me away from this land when I turned against our people. I was angry and hurt when my father died . . ." His voice trailed off.

"You lost respect for the Spirits and refused the bobcat as your Guardian. When you turned your back on the leadership of our society, the elders gathered to pray for you. Would you ever respect the traditions that uphold our heritage?" Grandfather lovingly put his hand on Terry's shoulder and continued.

"The elders finally had a vision as to what to do. You would be tested. Your restless spirit would be placed in that of an ordinary housecat, not the mighty bobcat. You would live in a city far from here as you wished to do.

"Would you like that kind of life better? What would happen if your city cat became separated from HIS family? Where would you go? Would the two of you join as allies or remain separate and at odds. It was not a simple matter."

"Mack, dear Mack!" Terry instantly reconnected with the profound relationship we had. "What a journey I ... we have been on, Grandfather, with so many helpers along the way! That amazing cat had no idea what he would be going through to help me. I tried to speak to him in dreams, but it only came out as nightmares for him. So, I tried to partner with him in actions. He kind of caught on sometimes . . . but I was struggling myself to find out what was important and what to do. Eventually we both joined in our mutual quest for the meaning of 'home.'"

The elders all nodded and spoke to him one by one.

"We prayed that you would fall back on the teachings of your forefathers, and help the cat make wise decisions and choices along the way. His innocence to Indian ways would be a real challenge."

"We prayed that you would be able to see your friends, the many creatures of this earth, as allies and guardians in the search for home."

"We were prepared to let you be lost to us forever, if that is what you truly wanted."

"We wanted to give you both every opportunity to return to us. Thankfully, you took them."

"There was much to accomplish in order to make it home. Going in all Four Directions was essential, as was learning the honorable qualities of Courage, Patience, Endurance, and Quick Thinking. Without the humbling influence of all of these, you would never have been able to accept the demands of the wilderness, nor hear the wisdom of our ancestors," finished Leonard.

A bit overwhelmed, Terry replied. "I have learned to respect the tradition of hunting. I am now grateful for the bounties of the land. I know now that I never meant to insult the dignity of our traditions, or the sacredness of our ancestors. I know now that I hold dear the rituals and beliefs that bind our clan. It is an honor to accept the bobcat as my Spirit Guide. Our encounter in the wilderness showed me the power of his protection.

Elders, I no longer want to live in a city. I just want to be able to live here, and balance the old with the new of the modern world. And please, where is Mack? I would not be here without him." Terry's affection for the chubby cat shone in his smiling, dark eyes.

Grandfather beamed in agreement. "We have honored the cat's remarkable abilities during this passage. We have blessed him with a new name from our people. Now, he is not only Mackenzie, but 'Nahtotse Nesemoo.'"

"Oh, WOW!" 'my pet, the friendly helping spirit'. What a tribute! And his family? Are they here?"

"Yes, Nesemoo was thrilled to find out that his family was actually here, living in a house near the place where the wind really does howl down from the mountains," Grandfather chuckled.

"Over by the hospital?"

"Yes, Bill Butler works in our medical clinic there. Julie and Jack are enrolled in our school, and June Butler is learning how to do beadwork from your mother! We are quite pleased that they are interested in learning about our culture. They are adjusting to the weather and the 'spirits' in the wind. I'm sure you will see them around town.

"You and Jack are almost the same age. You might go over there and introduce yourself, and meet their recently returned cat! Anyway, your mother has invited the Butler family to your Naming Ceremony tonight." Grandfather Leonard grinned with deep pride in his eyes.

"What?" Terry suddenly sat up straight. "Is it Pow Wow time?"

"Yes, it is almost the Moon of the Harvest Grass. You have been gone since the Moon of the New Grass. In these last months you have truly earned your status as a leader in our clan. Go now, and greet your family outside."

Terry respectfully acknowledged all of the elders before he left the tipi. Their voices filled him with confidence.

That evening, the last night of the yearly Pow Wow, both local residents and visitors gathered at the town's outdoor arena. My family sat in the bleachers with Terry's mother, Lucy, and many other of their relatives. I sat under the bleachers, beaming from whisker to whisker as I caught sight of Terry. He was all dressed up in his richly decorated Native regalia.

I listened intently as Lucy explained the meaning of many of their customs. I began to see in a new light many of the values that arose on our adventure. I felt a surge of alliance as I remembered how hard we had both worked to recognize the true meaning of 'home'. My family seemed curiously drawn to this Naming Ceremony, as though they had some baffling bond with this young man they had met only today. Would they ever know the truth of the matter?

I purred with embarrassment as Julie, Jack, William, and June all related their excitement at the sudden return of their beloved lost cat, who had somehow been separated during their trip to this town.

"A gift from the Great Spirit, no doubt," remarked Lucy candidly, as she winked toward me underneath.

Finally, the moment arrived. Grandfather Leonard thanked the Creator for Terry's safe and successful return to his people.

"Terry Makeeta (Littleman), your family is proud to announce a new name given to you this day: Tseske Veho (Small Chief Walksalone)." And the festivities lasted long into the night.

The next afternoon, while horseback riding with his grandfather on the prairie, Terry sadly confessed, "I sure miss Mack. I got so used to being with him everyday. He is a brave warrior and a worthy ally."

"Nesemoo was and still is a special blessing from the Creator. His unique spirit can continue to remind you, along with the bobcat, that to be a leader in our tribe, you must grow with wisdom, kindness, and generosity toward all people.

Some time in the future you may walk again with Nesemoo. For now, you must take what you have learned, and walk alone toward Tseske Veho, the man."

"All right," conceded Terry, and to himself he whispered, "See you, Nesemoo Mack, and thank you."

And that's the story as I know it. Terry comes over to play video games with Jack now and then. I always rub against his leg and purr, and he always picks me up and scratches my chin and the white patch at my throat.

For now, I am happy just roaming and hunting prairie dogs on the vast plain. Other than that, I like lounging on laps in the house. It's a cat thing, you know. See ya!

The End

References/Bibliography

Black Elk, Wallace and Lyon, William S, 1990. THE SACRED WAYS OF A LAKOTA.
San Francisco: HarperCollins.

Dictionary, Cheyenne. 1998. Lame Deer, Mt. Dull Knife Memorial College Library.

Hungry Wolf, Beverly, 1996. DAUGHTERS OF THE BUF-FALO WOMEN:MATNTAINING THE TRIBAL FAITH. Canada: Canadian Caboose Press.

Language Research Dept. of the Northern Cheyenne Bilin-gual Education Program. 1976. ENGLISH-CHEYENNE STU-DENT DICTIONARY. Lame Deer, MT: Dull Knife Memorial College Library.

Long Standing Bear Chief. 1992. NI-KSO-KO-WA: BLACK-FOOT SPIRITUALITY, TRADITIONS, VALUES and BE-LIEFS. Browning, MT. Spirit Talk Press.

Nettl, Bruno. 1989. BLACKFOOT MUSICAL THOUGHT.
Kent, Ohio: The Kent State Uni. Press.

Storm, Hyemeyohsts. 1972. SEVEN ARROWS.
New York, N.Y.: Harper and Row.

Printed in the United States
132993LV00002B/1-441/P